Book Club Edition

First American Edition. Copyright © 1980 by Walt Disney Productions.
All rights reserved under International and Pan-American Copyright
Conventions. Published in the United States by Random House, Inc.,
New York, and simultaneously in Canada by Random House of Canada
Limited, Toronto. Originally published in Denmark as FEDTMULE PROVER
LYKKEN by Gutenberghus Bladene, Copenhagen.
ISBN: 0-394-84627-3 (trade); 0-394-94627-8 (lib. bdg.)
Manufactured in the United States of America
1 2 3 4 5 6 7 8 9 0   A B C D E F G H I J K

WALT DISNEY PRODUCTIONS

presents

Goofy the Gardener Makes Up His Mind

Random House  New York

It was early in the morning.
Goofy was already at work.
He was a gardener.
Gardening was hard work but
Goofy enjoyed it.

Goofy watered the trees and flowers.
He trimmed the hedges, too.
He liked to make the gardens look
beautiful.

One hot day his friend Mickey stopped to say hello.

"What a hot day!" said Mickey.

Goofy stood up and wiped his forehead.
"Whew! It sure is hot," he said.
"It is too hot to be planting trees," said
Mickey. "You should find an easier job."

Hmm, an easier job, thought Goofy. Maybe
I am working too hard.

"Go to the supermarket tomorrow," said
Mickey. "The store owner needs help."

"Okay," said Goofy.
"Working in a supermarket
sounds easier."

The next morning
Goofy woke up early.
He combed his hair
carefully.

Then he headed for
the supermarket.

"Do you have a job for me, sir?"
Goofy asked.

"Yes, indeed!" said the store owner.
"Put on this apron and follow me."

He took Goofy to the storeroom.
Large boxes were piled to the ceiling.
"First," said the store owner,
"move all these boxes to the front of
the store. Then unpack them.
And then come and see me."

The store owner left Goofy with
all the boxes.

Goofy was surprised.
"I thought he would
help me! I am not sure
this is an easier job."
But he set to work.

"Uggh," groaned Goofy. "This box is heavy!"

He carried all the boxes to the front of the store.
One by one he unpacked them.
Goofy was very tired.

Bananas
33¢ a pound

Finally it was time to go home.
"I cannot wait to leave," said Goofy.

Just then the
store owner
returned.

"Wait," he said. "There are a few
more boxes. You cannot leave
until you unpack them."

The boxes were filled with many cans.
The store owner showed Goofy how to
stack the cans.

Finally Goofy left the supermarket.
It was dark out.

On his way home he met Donald Duck.
"You look tired, Goofy," said Donald.
"What have you been doing?"
Goofy told Donald about his job at the supermarket.
"You should find an easier job," said Donald.

Donald walked Goofy home.

"Go to Gino's Restaurant tomorrow," said Donald. "I know Gino needs some help."

"Gino's!" said Goofy. "Maybe that will be an easy place to work."

The next day Donald took Goofy to Gino's.
Goofy wanted to be the headwaiter.
So he wore his fanciest jacket.
"Gino," said Donald, "here is Goofy. He
wants to work for you."

"I am glad to meet you, Goofy," said Gino.
Goofy was pleased and excited.

"Have you ever worked in a restaurant?" asked Gino.

"No," said Goofy. "But I will learn what to do."

"Good," said Gino. "The first thing to do is put on our restaurant uniform."

"Now you really look like a waiter, Goofy," said Donald.

Then Gino said, "Now you are ready for work. You can start in the kitchen."

"First peel all these potatoes," said Gino.
Goofy never did get out of the kitchen.

He had to scrub the pots and mop the floor.
This is not easy at all, thought Goofy.

Goofy was finally ready to say good night.
"But, Goofy," said Gino, "you still have to
wash the dishes."

This is not easy either, Goofy said to himself.
"Good night, Goofy," the other workers said.

Finally Goofy finished his work.
It was very late.
He was so tired he could barely walk!

"What is the matter, Goofy?" called his friend Clarabelle. "Come in for a cup of tea and tell me all about it."

Goofy told her all about his new job.
"It sounds like very hard work to me,"
said Clarabelle. "Maybe I can find you
an easier job."

She read the help-wanted ads to Goofy.

"Listen," said Clarabelle. "A house painter
needs a helper. That will be an easy job for you."

Goofy's eyes lit up.

"Thanks, Clarabelle," he said. "You are
a real friend."

The next morning Goofy went
to see the house painter.

"Do you need a helper?"
he asked.

"I sure do," the man said.
"Hop in my truck!"

"Just do what I tell you," said the man.
"It is not hard."

The house was a mess!
"Fix the cracks first," said the man.

Goofy filled the cracks
with plaster.
Then he mixed the paint.

"Now paint the ceilings," the house painter told Goofy. "And do not make a mess!"

Then Goofy put up
the wallpaper...

and painted all the
window frames...

and patched up even more
holes in the walls!

Late in the afternoon the
house painter said good-bye.
He drove off in his truck.
Goofy had to walk home.
He walked very slowly!

On his way home, he passed Mickey.
Mickey was raking his lawn.

"Hi, Mickey," Goofy said.
"How are you?"

"Very tired," answered Mickey.
"Gardening is hard work. I do
not like it."

"Gosh, I still like gardening," said Goofy.

"I will come help you in the morning."

"Gee, thanks," said Mickey.

Early the next morning Goofy started
working in Mickey's garden.
He planted some flowers.
He picked others that were in bloom.

He mowed the lawn.
He trimmed the hedges, too.

By the end of the day, Mickey's garden looked beautiful.

Goofy was tired but he felt good.

He sat down and admired his day's work.

And then he sang this song:
I paid the price of friends' advice
And worked at jobs I did not like.
But now I will work even harder
And be who I am—Goofy the gardener!